The Freaky Joe Club

The Freaky Joe Club

Secret File #1:
The Mystery of the Swimming Gorilla

Secret File #2:
The Case of the Smiling Shark

Illustrated by
John Manders

The Freaky Joe Club

Secret File #3:

The Mystery of the Morphing Hockey Stick

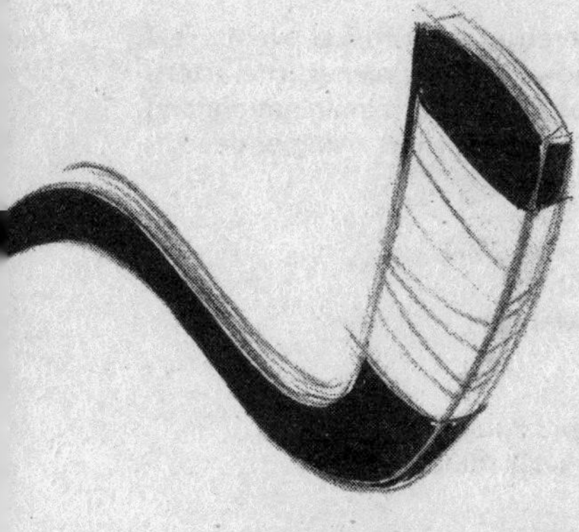

by
P. J. McMahon

ALADDIN PAPERBACKS
New York London Toronto Sydney

To the amazing Emily,
who knows Mugsy very well
— P. J. M.

First Aladdin Paperbacks edition September 2004

ALADDIN PAPERBACKS
An imprint of Simon & Schuster Children's Publishing Division
1230 Avenue of the Americas, New York, NY 10020

Designed by Lisa Vega
The text of this book was set in 14-point Minion.
Printed in the United States of America
10 9 8 7 6 5 4 3 2 1

Library of Congress Control Number 2004102672
ISBN 0-689-86262-8

Table of Contents

Chapter One

A Squire! A Squire?

Here I am, again. Alone in The Secret Place, with my thoughts, my memories, and with a chewed-up pencil in my mouth. The Red Book, the actual, real, and true Secret Files of the Freaky Joe Club, lies open in my lap. *Shark! Octopi!* The words seem to leap off the pages as I read the ending of an earlier adventure. An ant staggers out of the book. An ant that has clearly survived on dog biscuit crumbs.

Riley, my dog and the official Beast of this Freaky Joe Club, lifts her head. Wonders if the ant is worth chasing or eating. Decides no. Resumes chewing the laces of my skates.

My skates. The roller blades lie side by side. Where there should be wheels, there are none. New green wheels sit waiting to be placed on the skates. First I'll finish this task, then the skates.

Hockey skates. These are at the heart of the tale that now must be told. So that one day the truth will be revealed. And one day the bravery and cunning of the Freaky Joe Club will be known to all.

Where to begin? Where to begin? In the dark heart of a building called the Alamo.

Nah. That comes later in my story. One afternoon, as a hot Texas summer is coming to an end . . .

. . . A brave knight rides on over hills and dales and through a dark day. Sir Chester the Clever, Knight Detective, searches for the one clue that will solve the mystery. What vile fiend stole the Sacred Saracen Sword of Stonehenge Castle? Sir Chester knows that he alone can solve this crime. Aided, of course, by his loyal squire, Chuck.

There is nothing like a good mystery.

"Hark!" Sir Chester calls to Chuck. "From whence cometh that foul noise?"

BUZZ! BUZZ! BUZZ! BUZZ!

The foul noise spreadeth from the book throughout the Secret Place. With loud barks Riley objects to the noise.

What is up? Is the secret home of the Freaky Joe Club under attack? Leaping to my feet, I conduct an investigation. My keen detective skills lead me to the windowsill. Where I discover that some vile fiend has left a loudly buzzing kitchen timer.

Leaping to her feet, Riley grabs the alarm before I can.

"Give it to me, you varlet! You dread hound!" Grabbing my lance, the hockey stick of doom, I give chase.

While chasing the Beast, I remember words spoken not a short time ago.

"You have to put that book down and get ready," my mother said as she stood in the door of The Secret Place. Car keys jangled in her hand.

"It is not That Book. It is the third book in the series The Adventures of Sir Chester the Clever, Knight Detective." I had to find something to read while waiting for the thirteenth Remington Reedmarsh to come out.

"You need to put down the third book in the

series The Adventures of Sir Chester the Clever, Knight Detective, or you will be late," my mother said.

"Is it good?" she added.

"Very. And I promise," I answered as she left.

"We'll see," she answered.

My keen memory has solved this mystery.

"She didn't trust me, Riley," I tell The Beast as I wrestle the timer from her great jaws.

Good thing. I'm going to be so late.

My armor lies scattered around our headquarters. Now I am the one dressing for battle.

Shin guards wrap around my legs. My helmet leans on the thick gloves, which will protect my hands as I hold the wooden hockey stick of battle.

I'll put them on last. Just as soon as, just as soon as . . .

"Aaargggghhh." I let loose with the well-known cry of the frustrated person.

With my head up under my arm, I try to reach the back strap of my chest protector to hook it to the front strap. Then I'll be ready to meet my boon companions. Except I keep dropping it at the last minute. Over and over again.

Now I know why Sir Chester always has Chuck around. Besides the fact that Chuck spots clues before anyone. Because without Chuck, Sir Chester would spend all his time in his tent fussing with straps while tournaments took place and dragons ran around destroying villages.

"Hold on, I'll be with you in a minute" is not exactly

going to work with Evil Knights or destructor dragons.

Stop, Conor. Take a breath. You cannot play hockey with your head stuck in an armpit. You can do this, I tell myself. But a squire would be handy right about now.

At that moment, a strange wind blows open the door to The Secret Place. Seeming to come straight from the setting sun, a figure appears in the room.

"Ta da!" it cries. Stops. Stares at me. Then begins to speak again.

Sometimes wishes come true.

Sometimes magical squires appear at your door, ready to help.

Chapter Two

A Jack! A Jack!

And other times . . .

"Why have you got your head stuck under your pits? Why aren't you ready? Are we going to play, or what? I left my stuff out in the driveway. But I'm all ready, look! Why aren't you ready? It's Hockey Time! Don't you know we have an important game in like one minute? What's taking so long? I was ready in two minutes. I am ready to roll."

Jack stops for a brief breath. He snaps his fingers in rhythm as he repeats, "Let's go. Let's go. Let's go."

Yes, sometimes wishes do come true. And sometimes, Jack shows up. Jack, holder of many land-speed records and secret agent of the Freaky Joe Club.

"I know we have a game. That's why I'm putting on my stuff," I explain while reaching for the strap again.

"I can't hear you; you have your head up your armpit," Jack answers. He comes around behind me to hear better. Which gives me a wonderful close-up of his face. Upside down.

"Hand me that strap, so I don't have to look up your nose anymore," I say.

"What's it look like?" Jack continues to stare while he hands the strap to me. Then he begins to skate circles around The Secret Place with Riley following.

I pull on my jersey and smooth down the picture of the scary, green, dangerous creature on the front. A hockey team should have just the right logo.

Almost ready now, I ask, "Where's Timmy?"

"He's coming." Jack tries to spins on one roller

blade. Riley tries to bite it as he turns. "We were coming together but he had to carry that heavy bag, so he got left behind. Not as fast as me." Jack crouches down in a speed skater position. Riley lines up alongside.

"Tell Riley to stop copying me," Jack asks.

"Why didn't you help?" I ask.

Jack looks at me as if I have two heads and both of them are stuck up my pits. "Then I wouldn't have been the first one to get here," he explains. "And that would be no good."

I grab my helmet and stick. "Be a good girl, Riley," I tell her. "Guard The Secret Place."

"And don't eat anyone's flesh," Jack suggests.

We race to the end of the driveway as Timmy arrives lugging an enormous bag. Which he drops on the ground as he collapses on top.

Timmy is the third secret agent of the Freaky Joe Club. And our team goalie.

"Thanks for helping me, Jack," he mumbles into the bag.

"Why is everyone making it so hard for me to hear them today?" Jack asks.

"Where is my mom?" is the question I ask. We need to be at the hockey rink in time to warm up. And she isn't in the driveway as she said she would be. "She promised she'd be back here in a minute after she dropped Bella off and picked Murphy up."

"If we don't have Murphy, we can't play. And that would be bad," Jack says, pointing out the obvious. He is very good at this.

A roller hockey team has to have five players to compete. We have five players.

"We also have to have your mom," Timmy tells me, which I already know.

"What color is she today?" Jack pretends to be a painter, making wide brush strokes as he paints the sky. This lasts for a minute before he starts making skating jumps over the collapsed Timmy.

"She was blue last time I saw her," I confess. I hope she is less blue for the game. My mother is a painter who tends to wear her work around. She is also the coach of our roller hockey team. Not that she knows much about the game. She doesn't. But I do. And every team has to have an adult or high school student as a coach. Which I'm not. So it works.

Timmy lifts only one arm. Grabs Jack's ankle as he flies over. Which causes Jack to crash.

"Hey! You could kill me!" Jack screams.

"You're killing me," Timmy screams as Jack lands on him.

"Guys, we cannot win our game with both of you smashed," I remind them.

"Do you think we can win?" Timmy asks through Jack's armpit.

"No doubt at all," I swear. Freaky Joe Rule Number Eighteen: Be Confident. It Can't Hurt.

"We don't win a lot," Jack points out.

"We won our last three games," I remind him. "We keep getting better and better."

"What I wonder," Timmy says, "is what we're doing different that makes us win?" He fishes around in his jersey, with the same bloodthirsty creature on the front. "I'm starving." He unfolds a napkin filled with green crumbs. And happily begins to munch.

"Anyone want some?" he offers.

"What is it?" Jack leans over for a look.

"I can't remember," Timmy confesses. "It's green now."

"Big no!" Jack backs up quickly.

"Guys, remember. A win tonight and we enter the summer league play-offs. We're in the race for first place. We could be the champions."

I hold my stick high above my head. I skate a

victory lap singing the champions' song. Jack joins me. I do my famous Balancing on One Skate glide. Timmy throws green crumbs in the air.

"Here comes your mom," Timmy yells.

I see our big, green, sorta new car/truck thing heading our way. Well, it's not new, just new to us. My mom wants to paint designs on it. This is worrisome. I mean, just one time maybe we could blend in.

"Grab your gear, men. We ride into battle. And we shall emerge victorious."

"You're reading a book again, aren't you?" Jack asks.

My mom pulls into the driveway.

"How are we going to fit?" Jack wonders.

"Hey, little guys!" Timmy calls.

I look. Oh no, oh no!

Chapter Three

Remember the Alamo?

"Mom, how could you?" I ask her. Okay, I shout at her through the open window.

"Hey, Conor! Hey, Jack! Hey, Timmy!" my sister, Bella, calls out. From inside the truck where she is *not* supposed to be. She is supposed to be at Mugsy's house so my mom can coach my team in this all-important game.

"Conor, can I play? Can I? Can I? Can I?" Mugsy calls from where she is sitting next to Bella. "I'm as good as Murphy."

Mugsy's older sister, Murphy, rolls her eyes. Murphy is one of the reasons our team is doing well. Big sister can skate.

"You guys look good," Mugsy's little brother, Mikey, says. "I like your shirts," he adds. "Green is my favorite color."

"Then have a crumb," Timmy offers. Mikey happily accepts.

"Is Dwayne playing?" Jack whispers in my ear. "That would be kinda bad."

Kinda bad, since Dwayne has trouble walking. But clearly he has no trouble sitting, as that is what he is doing right now. Sitting here!

"Hop in, gentlemen," my mom announces. "There is a hockey game awaiting."

Timmy and Jack climb in, over and around the little kids.

"Mom! You were supposed to leave Bella, not bring her back with more kids," I remind her as I climb in front.

"Couldn't be helped. Their mom got called to work. And she was watching Dwayne. They won't cause any trouble," my mom promises.

"They always cause trouble."

"They can sit on the bench and draw," she explains.

"No! No! No! No!" I try to make my feelings clear. "They can't draw. They cannot sit on the players' bench."

"Calm down," my mother suggests. "I'll sit them where I can see them and set them up with crayons and paper. What could be the problem?" she asks. "Mugsy, please stop doing what

you're doing. It isn't polite and could cause a major accident."

"How major?" Mugsy wants to know.

What could be the problem? We finally have a chance to show that this big, bad, mean, green machine can play hockey. One more win and we are in the play-offs. For the first time ever.

So we need to concentrate. Not be distracted. Not have to answer questions like, Do unicorns skate? And why do we use a stick anyway? And have we ever made anyone bleed?

So I asked my mother for one little favor: to not bring my little sister, Bella, not to mention her friends, to the game. Just one itty bitty little request of a mother by her son. A son who never ever asks for anything. Who never complains no matter what big ideas his mother has. Like making paintings as big as our walls, or, say, flying off to China to adopt the little sister who is not supposed to come to this hockey game.

But does this mother leave the little sister behind? Very big no. Instead she brings along the sister and her best friend, who is likely to be the first five-year-old elected to the Evil Genius Club.

"Okay, here we are. Everyone unload. Let's play some hockey!" My mother does that cheery thing adults do when they know you're upset, and it's their fault, but nothing is going to change.

"Let's hurry," I urge everyone. "We're running late."

"I'm the first one in the door," Jack calls as he leaps out the door. Unfortunately Dwayne moves at the same time.

I untangle them.

"Mugsy, climb down off the roof," my mother orders. "It's bad manners to walk on my car."

"I'll carry a stick," Bella says. She rides the stick in a circle. "I'm Beautiful Belinda on Baby Katie the Unicorn."

Dwayne trips over the stick.

"We have to get going," I announce to everyone.

"Right away, sweetie," my mom answers. "Dwayne, take this stick. Mugsy, it's bad manners to walk on any cars."

Dwayne trips over his own stick.

Timmy and Mikey are still in the car eating.

"We're going to miss the game," I tell the air.

Jack has Dwayne show him how the stick moved by itself.

"Come on, Conor, let's go." Bella takes my hand. "This is an important game."

What a smart kid. It must be thanks to her big brother.

"I don't like that man on the roof," Bella confesses as we

reach the front door. "I think he's going to fall on my head."

"He's not going to fall on your head. I won't let him," I promise. "Besides, he's one of the good guys. He's fighting for Texas."

We both stop to look up at the soldier defending the roof of the roller-skating rink. My team plays here at the Siege of the Alamo Roller Hockey Rink. The outside has been painted and wooden cutouts have been added to the roof so the building looks exactly like the real Alamo. On the roof are several brave wooden defenders

who appear to be aiming their cardboard rifles at Big Bertha's Boots and Bangles store across the street.

One fellow has been hit bad, and leans way off the roof, about to die for our cause. Or land on Bella's head.

As we enter the door to the rink, the others catch up with us. My mom has Mugsy in what appears to be a walking headlock.

The owner of the rink greets us we come in. "Ah, Ship's Cove people! There you are. I was beginning to worry!"

"Why are you dressed like that?" Mugsy asks, her voice a little funny. Maybe she could use a little more oxygen.

"She's William Travis," Timmy and I answer at the exact same time.

"Now I can't understand Mugsy," Jack complains. "There's something funny going on."

There is nothing funny about Timmy and me

knowing the answer. Jamie Bowie Boudreaux, owner of the rink, dresses every day as one of the daring leaders of the brave men who fought and died at the Alamo.

I'm quoting here.

After a while, it is pretty easy to tell Travis from Jim Bowie and Davy Crockett. The outfits are real and true copies of what they wore. Well, except for the skates. She always wears skates. But sometimes adds a bandage or two.

Big Buster, the referee, races over to us. "So, Ship's Cove decided to show after all," he says.

"I told you not to worry," Miz Boudreaux reminds him.

"Sometimes a big game comes up and a team gets scared," Buster tells us.

"Buster, I know this is big," she says. "But if you want to talk about an important Monday evening, I can think of one in 1863. . . ."

As good a story as the Alamo is, we don't have time right now. I interrupt.

"We're not scared," I tell Buster. "We came to win."

"Do you think you can? Let's see how the Big Green Machine does." Buster skates away, jumping over three hockey bags and one little brother. And knocking down one adult.

"WHATTAYA THINK YOU'RE DOING? ARE YOU TRYING TO MESS WITH ME?" the grown-up yells from the floor.

"Oh no, the Howler is here," Timmy says as Buster stands her up and dusts her off.

"WATCH OUT, BUSTER!" The owner of the voice takes a swing at the ref, who is already skating away.

"Man, I forgot to bring cotton," Jack says.

"I think there's some in the bottom of my bag," Timmy says.

"I think there are new life-forms evolving in the bottom of your bag." Jack laughs hard at his own joke.

"And they will be smarter than this life-form here," Timmy answers.

I sense a battle looming. We have no time for skirmishes. As captain of the team, I must act.

Before I can speak, a shout rings through the building.

Chapter Four

Beached Whales Eat Candy?

"You guys, you guys, where have you been? Hurry up." Mad Dog, whose mother named him Charley, races up at a pretty impressive land-speed record. He makes a screeching, full-side skating stop. Which causes Dwayne to fall down again. Even though Mad Dog was nowhere near Dwayne.

"It's almost equipment check time," Mad Dog insists. "And we haven't even warmed up."

"And I have to get all this stuff on." Timmy collapses next to Dwayne under the weight of his bag.

"Go, go," my mom urges. "I'll be along in a second. Right after I explain some very important facts to some lovely children." She gives the little guys a truly evil eye.

Jack, Murphy, and Mad Dog speed off.

Dwayne tries to play dead.

"We are all going to be oh so good, aren't we, lovely little children?" my mom asks. "Cause not trouble? Rearrange not the furniture? Scale not the walls?"

"Oh yes," Bella says. She uses one hand to push Mugsy's head up and down.

Timmy and I drag his bag. We pass the cannons outside the video games section of the rink. And the Howler, who is talking with her son Gavin, who plays for the other guys.

"NO VIDEO GAMES NOW! NO MACHINES UNTIL YOU WIN! GO SKATE!"

I have the idea that I should tell my mother she is a pretty good mother. Even if she is blue.

Timmy and I dodge balls and skaters as we

cross the floor to the players' benches on the other side of the rink. Jack, Murphy, and Mad Dog warm up, shooting the smooth red ball into the open net.

At the other end, the other team shoots well. Their goalie blocks shots.

We can do this, I tell myself. I try hard to believe myself. I mean, it is just a simple hockey game. What could go wrong?

I try not to think about Freaky Joe Rule Number Five: Something Always Goes Wrong. That's the Point.

The Howler screams, "GO! GO! SHOOT THAT BALL! BE AGGRESSIVE!" And the game hasn't started yet.

Timmy pulls his stuff out of the bag. The giant pads seem to fight back. Candy wrappers and odd-colored round somethings fly out.

"Conor, I'm good to go." Timmy lays his very wide pads on the floor and flops on top, and I tighten the straps. Timmy's job is to keep any balls from rolling into the net. So he wears these gigantic leg pads. Which block a whole bunch of space. Which is good. But once he has them on, Timmy can hardly move at all. Which is not so good.

Right now he looks exactly like a beached whale.

"Okay. On the count of three, I pull and you push up," I tell him. "One. Two. Uummphh."

Timmy is not up. And I am now down.

I scramble to my feet. The other team is lined up by their bench watching.

"Jack, come here," I call.

"Jack-man to the rescue." Jack races over, does the screeching hockey side stop. Which has never been his best move. He loses his balance. Grabs my jersey. Goes down. Taking me with him.

I now have my head in Jack's armpit.

We are not striking fear into the hearts of our enemy.

The enemy applauds. Their coach says, "Focus. Does everyone have his gloves? Gavin, you forgot them last time."

Gavin waves his gloves at his coach. Waves them backward at us.

"What does that mean?" Jack cracks his knuckles hard. That'll scare 'em.

"That's an ancient greeting used by knights before a joust," I tell him. We still have no time for skirmishes.

Together we pull Timmy upright. Wheel him to the net. And turn him around so he faces the right way.

"Okay, let 'er rip," I tell my team. Red balls fly at Timmy. Too many fly or roll past him into the net.

Which is in that Not Good category.

My mother jogs across the floor, clapping her

hands loudly. "Let's go! Big game! Big game!"

Jack skates around her shouting "Big game! Big game!"

On the sidelines, Bella, Mugsy, Mikey, and Dwayne jump up and down yelling "Big game!"

I think everyone gets the idea.

"Uh, Mom, what are you doing?" I ask her as she pounds me on my helmet.

"Just trying to be coachlike," she answers, pounding Timmy on the back. "Big Timmy!" she shouts.

He falls face forward.

"Big Timmy, Big Timmy!" our four fans yell.

"Pick him up, please," I beg my teammates.

"Pick him up! Pick him up!" Our fans manage a four-person wave. Dwayne falls backward.

"Are we ready?" Coach Mom asks.

"Could you check everyone's equipment?" I ask. No equipment, no play is the rule. "I need to talk to Timmy."

"Timmy." I lift his helmet so he can hear me. "I overheard the guys on the other team talking. They said you couldn't block anything."

"I can block some things," Timmy protests.

"They said scoring on you is like taking candy from a baby. Like stealing a lollipop from Dwayne. They said if all the candy in the world was in that net, they could eat forever."

"They think they can take my candy?" Timmy looks serious. Smacks one big glove into another. Which makes him wobble.

"They do, they do. But I know they can't," I promise him, holding him upright. "I know you will protect it. Just imagine, Timmy, that every red ball rolling toward you is a bomb. A bomb that will blow up all your candy unless you stop it."

"I'll stop them!"

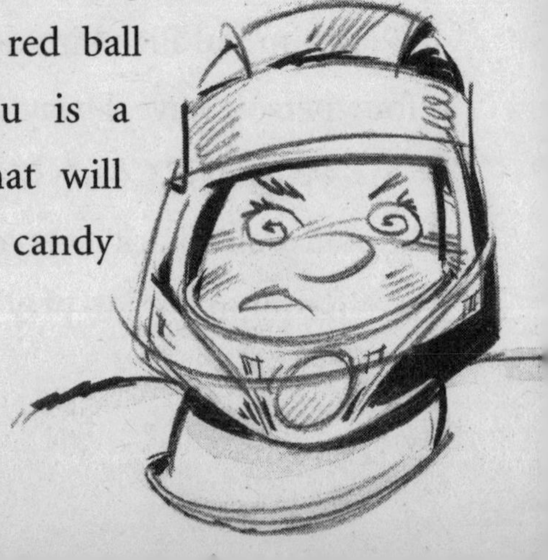

Timmy shouts. It could be the light, but I swear his eyes begin to glow red.

And at that moment, all the lights go out.

"It's starting," Murphy says into the darkness.

"I am ready," Mad Dog answers.

"I am Hockey Man," Jack declares.

"Must save candy," Timmy says in a zombielike voice.

"Hey, watch it," I call as someone skates right into me in the dark. I manage to keep Timmy and me upright.

"Watch out what?" Jack calls on one side of me.

"Huh?" Mad Dog asks on the other.

All I get is a grunt from the skater.

"That's okay, don't say excuse me," I call out.

No one answers.

"The Yellow Rose of Texas" finishes playing over the P.A.

The darkness begins to fade.

Chapter Five

What Was the Question?

One light—a disco ball turning slowly—comes on over the center of the rink. Loud music cranks on, with the words "Pump it up," repeated over and over.

"HOCKEY!" the Howler screams.

"Lollipops. Gummy worms," Timmy drones.

Big Buster skates to the middle. He leaps and turns, showing just what can be done on roller blades. His black-and-white referee shirt blurs as he twirls under the light.

"I can do that," Jack declares.

"No, you can't," everyone reminds him.

"ARE YOU READY FOR SOME HOCKEY?" Buster screams over the music.

"Yes!" the skaters yell.

"YES! YES! YES!" The Howler jumps up and down, yelling.

Bella and Mugsy jump up and down, yelling, "Crazy Lady! Crazy Lady!"

"ARE YOU READY?" Buster screams out.

Didn't we just say yes?

You know, this seems simple to me. Here we are, in this building, wearing helmets, pads, jerseys, skates, and holding long sticks. I think any reasonable person would look at us and say, These kids are ready to play some hockey.

But we're talking about Big Buster. Who wears skates that light up on the side, spelling out the name of the sport. He skates around and around the rink shouting "Are you ready to play some hockey?"

I believe we answered the question.

Jack and Mad Dog scream, "Yes!"

Timmy yells, "It's my candy!"

My mother yells "Hoo! Hoo!" I wonder where she read that a coach should imitate owls.

"I can't hear you!" Buster calls. Which is odd, because they can hear us on Henderson Island off the coast of Madagascar, which has a human population of six and a rare lemur population of forty-two.

"What's wrong with your ears? They said yes!" a voice calls out even louder. Well, all right, Mugsy!

Buster takes his place under the light. "Hockey Fans, tonight's lineup. From Merrie Old England, give it up for the London Gentlemen."

The other team skates out to the howls of one of their fans.

"GO GET 'EM," she screams. "RIP THEM APART!"

Our opponents did not cross the wide Atlantic to be here tonight. They live in Merrie Old England, the neighborhood across from Sylvan Glen. The one with the castle at the entrance.

They wear red jerseys with gold buttons down the front and those fringy things on their shoulders. Epaulets. Their helmets have crowns painted on them.

I would move to Henderson Island before I played for that team.

The London Gentlemen just does not seem like a hockey name. I look down at the mean green guy on my jersey. This is a fierce creature, a true representative of the sport. My mother drew the picture.

The coach of the other team marches up and down past his lined-up players. He wears a fancy jacket and a top hat. I don't even want to talk about it.

"We are gentlemen," he yells at them. "We have come to play and play well. And if in doing so, we destroy the enemy, well, that's just how it is done. It is the British Way. Take no quarter, men. Fight the good fight. Now parade attention, arms inspection."

I would like to point out that their coach is Tony, the guy who delivers for Speed's Pizza. Who came to Texas from Merrie Old New York. Who normally begins all sentences with the word "yo."

"And their opponents tonight come from the neighborhood of Ship's Cove. Hockey fans, please welcome the Bullfrogs!"

Murphy, Mad Dog, and Jack do a fancy fast skate out. Coach Mom and I push Timmy ahead of us. He holds his big goalie stick in front of him and bats away imaginary attackers.

"My candy cane. Mine."

I may have overdone it.

There are no crowns on our dark green helmets.

On our jerseys, a bullfrog, looking as mean as his species is, sits in front of crossed hockey sticks with his helmet on the lily pad in front of him.

"BULLFROGS? BULLFROGS?" the Howler yells out.

"Just who is that woman?" My mother turns, hands on hips.

"Mom, ignore her. You have to stay here and give us a pep talk," I explain.

"Okay team, huddle." My mom pulls everyone in a circle. I don't have time to tell her that hockey players don't huddle. "Let's win this game. And show them what's what. And kick some, you know, stuff. And do not listen to ignorant people who try to cover up their foolish lack of knowledge by making more noise than anyone else." This last bit was said, oh, a bit louder than the rest, and she didn't seem to be looking in our direction. "Remember, big game! Big game!"

"WHAT KIND OF TEAM IS NAMED BULL-FROGS?"

"You take it from here, Conor," my mom says. "I just need to check on your sister."

Who happens to be sitting next to a certain fan.

"I want to go watch this," Jack says.

I intercept. "You have to stay with us for inspection. It's the rule."

We stand in a line. Big Buster skates around us.

"Shin guards, helmets, gloves, elbow pads, neck pads. Check, check, check, check, and check. You guys look ready."

Please don't ask us for what.

He skates over to the London Gentlemen, who are standing at attention. Tony salutes Buster.

"Ready for parade, sir."

Buster inspects.

"COULD WE HAVE SOME HOCKEY, PLEASE," comes an oh-so-lovely voice from the sidelines.

"We have a problem here," Buster says to Tony. "One kid with no gloves."

"I have them; I just forgot." Gavin races to the bench. Looks around wildly. Yells, "Who took my gloves?"

"Who took Gavin's gloves?" Tony yells.

"SOMEONE TOOK MY KID'S GLOVES?" The Howler runs out onto the rink.

"Are fans allowed on the court?" my mom asks. "Shouldn't she be thrown out of the building? I could help."

Buster tells the Howler to find a seat. I don't tell my mom that the playing surface is not called a court.

I do ask her to hold Timmy. This should keep her in one place.

Tony orders his team to find the gloves.

"I hate to see a team lose this way," Buster says as he skates over. "But it looks like a big victory for the Bullfrogs."

"Bullfrogs. Bullfrogs," Jack begins to chant.

"Jack, cut it out," I say. "They'll find them. We both saw Gavin with his gloves."

The London Gentlemen do not act their name. They're pushing, shoving, looking, emptying bags, accusing each other of taking the gloves.

"Have you found them?" Buster calls out.

"Yo! Hold your horses," Tony yells.

"Not looking good for them," Buster tells us. "I think I'm standing with the big winners."

"We can really win without playing?" Mad Dog asks.

"If they don't have five players with full equipment, they are disqualified. They forfeit, you win," he explains. "Pretty good, eh?"

"Pretty bad," I answer. "That's not winning."

"That's your way into the play-offs," Buster promises.

"It is not our only way," I answer. "We're in if we win."

"If you can," Buster says. "Think you can?"

"We would get a trophy this big." Jack measures his hand from the floor.

"I don't want that trophy," I answer.

"What?" Buster and Jack ask.

"I don't want a trophy for lucking out," I tell them.

"Yeah," says Murphy.

"NOBODY TAKES MY KID'S GLOVES."

"Bullfrogs! Ribbit! Bullfrogs! Ribbit," Mugsy, Bella, Mikey, and Dwayne yell. They hop around like . . . like . . . well, bullfrogs.

"Take my chocolate? Take my gummies?" Timmy moans, still wobbling. He waves attackers away with his glove.

His big goalie's glove.

Ta da! I say to myself.

"Oh, Buster," I call out loud.

Chapter Six

Gumdrops, Kitty Cats, and Mad Girls

"Don't worry, kid, I'll declare you winners in a minute." Buster waves me off with the back of his hand. "We have to give them a fair chance," he says with a smile. Buster's a fair guy.

"I can help," I tell Buster. Banging on Timmy's helmet, I ask, in a loud voice, "Timmy, can you hear me? This is Conor calling."

"Conor?" Timmy's eyes begin to focus.

Jack rushes over. "Let me help. Timmy, how many times am I hitting you on the head?" Jack bangs his helmet.

"How many times am I going to hit you back?" Timmy asks.

Amazing. Jack actually helped.

"Timmy, do you have your regular hockey gloves with you?" I ask.

"They're in my bag."

"Can I get them?"

"Go ahead. Careful of my candy." And his eyes begin to glow again. "My candy! Are you trying to take my candy?"

"Jack, hold him upright. I'll look in his equipment bag." I skate away knowing that even if Timmy wanted to tackle me, he can't. 'Cause he can't move.

Timmy's bag has fallen over, so it's half on the bench, half on the floor. I open the zipper and peer inside. And realize what I have just said I would do. Look in Timmy's bag? What was I thinking? I might as well have said I'd go jump in a pool of toxic goo.

Looking for the gloves requires placing my face near the opening. *And* putting my hands *into* the bag. Down into the bag. Filled with . . . with . . . I can't think about it.

I hold it open wide. Look in sideways. Move closer. Nothing attacks me. Slowly I put my hand in, waving my fingers around. Then count. I still have five. Moving several plastic bags around, I find one glove. And another. One of the bags bumps away on its own. I swear.

And then I see it.

Uh-oh.

I drop the gloves back in for a second. Check to see if I am right about what I am looking at.

I am.

Oh boy.

Making sure I have the right two gloves, I quickly zip up the bag. I decide to follow Freaky Joe Rule Number Eleven D: Sometimes Things Have to Wait.

Even a mystery that needs to be solved.

"Hey, Mr. Tony," I call, waving the gloves over my head. "I have some gloves for Gavin."

"YOU TOOK MY KID'S GLOVES?"

"These are Timmy's gloves." I hand them to Gavin. "See, he has his name right on them." And many small pieces of peppermint candy stuck to them.

"Hey. Like, thanks," Gavin says.

"Well then, gentlemen," Tony announces, "we shall move forward thanks to this stouthearted fellow."

I rejoin my team.

"No big trophy?" Jack asks.

"Oh, big trophy," I promise. "Because we are going to win this game." How, I'm not sure. But I have a few ideas up my sleeve.

"Big game! Big game!" My mom says her line.

"Ribbit! Ribbit!" our fans cry.

"You do realize what you've done, don't you?" Buster asks.

"Yes, I do," I answer. "Now we're ready to play some hockey!"

If one desires to be a great coach, the secret is to help each player see that his job, or hers, is important. The team becomes a fighting machine when each member understands what is on the line today.

At least that is what the great Grady Li says in his book *The Chinese Martial Arts Guide to Roller Hockey.* I have the coaches' edition.

To play roller hockey, a team needs five players. First, and Mr. Li says most important, is the goalie.

"Gumdrops!"

We got that one covered.

We play one person, Mad Dog, on defense, and three on offense.

"Do not focus on playing defense. Trust your goalie and put your energy into scoring goals. That's the way to play Chinese Martial Roller Hockey," says Grady Li.

"Jellybeans."

Trust your goalie?

Mad Dog must keep the other guys from an easy run at the goal. And intercept the ball. And shoot it back down to the other end.

Jack, Murphy, and I are the offense. Our job is to bring the ball to their goal, then put it in the net to score. And then race back to help near our goal.

A lot of skating. This is good.

"One minute to start," Buster announces.

"Huddle again," my mom calls.

"There's some stuff I heard when I was lending them the gloves," I tell the team. "Stuff I think you should know. That kid Rodriquez, he says they are going to score a million points. 'Cause we have no defense."

"What does he mean, no D?" Mad Dog starts to snarl like . . . well, like a dog. A dog who is, well, mad.

"They laughed when I said to watch out for Mad Dog. 'He's no Mad Dog,' they said, 'he's more like a sweet little kitty cat.'" I'm sure that's what they mumbled. I couldn't quite understand.

"Kitty! Kitty!" Mad Dog is not happy.

"They probably remember when you were riding around on that Kissy Kitty bicycle," Jack points out. So helpful.

"Aaarrrggghhhh!" Mad Dog yells.

"They also said no one on our team is fast enough to catch them. 'Ha, we have a guy who sets land-speed records,' I said."

"And that is a fact 'bout Jack," says Jack.

"But not one they were buying. 'Maybe if he's racing a slug,' that's what they told me." Or what I might have heard.

"They didn't say anything about me?" Murphy asks, tucking her hair into the helmet.

"Only that you didn't count. 'Cause you're a girl."

Murphy pulls the visor over her face and smiles. “Well, we’ll just have to see about that.”

“Slug?”

“Kissy Kitty?”

“Girls don’t count?”

“Pink Bubble Gum!”

Well. I guess we are ready to play.

Chapter Seven

The First Battle at the Alamo

Buster stands in center rink, holding the ball high. Gavin and I wait, nose-to-nose, our sticks ready. Which is why this is called a face-off.

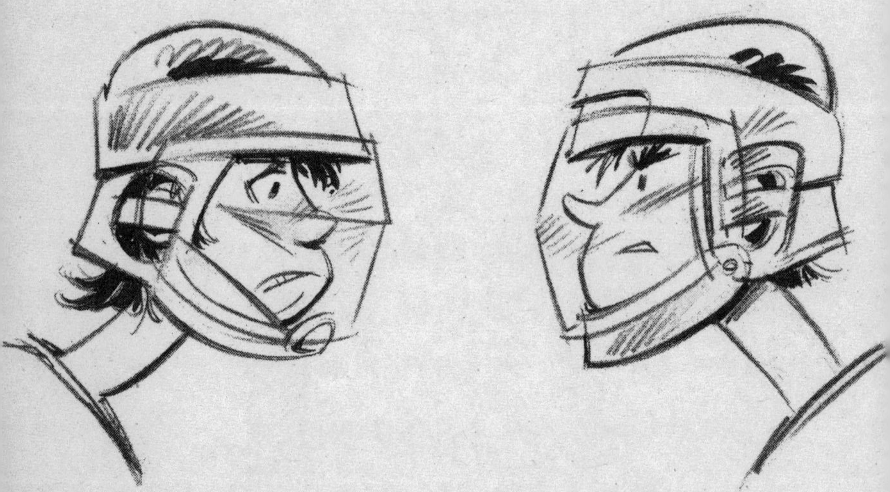

He drops it. I connect and shoot it off to Murphy.

She skates as fast as can be toward the other goal. I race up, and bang my stick to say I'm ready. She passes. The goalie comes out to block me. I shoot hard left.

He stops it.

"OH YEAH! OH BABY! OH YEAH! OH BABY!"

Oh man.

Ah, well. It was a good stop. Try again.

Another face-off. Off we go, up and down the rink. Trying to make it happen. Trying to score a goal.

The London Gentlemen try to do the same. But anytime they get near Mad Dog he yells, "Little Kitty?" or "Fur ball? You want a fur ball?" He barks loudly and shoots it away.

It unnerves them.

Timmy waves his stick around.

"Little square fruit candy!"

So far so good.

Not quite so good with Jack. He's not as focused as he could be.

"You want fast? I'll show you fast," he calls out to anyone who gets near him. And then races up and down the rink. It doesn't matter if he knows where the ball is at all.

I know where it is. What I love about hockey is the big picture. Where's the ball? Where's their defender? Are my teammates in position? (Jack's a no.) What's going to happen next?

Can I figure it out? Can I be in the right place at the right time?

It's like solving mysteries.

Right now I observe a London Gentleman, that Rodriquez, who has the ball. I steal it. Quick pass to Murphy. She turns fast and streaks toward the goal. They can't stop her. Big sister can skate. She's all alone in front of the goal. The goalie flops low. Murphy lifts the ball high.

And scores!

The Bullfrogs skate small victory circles.

"Girls rule! Boys drool!" our fans all cry. As does our coach. Our coach?

"You got that right!" Murphy yells.

But the Gentlemen get it back. Gavin gets past Mad Dog, who is busy barking at someone else. And finds that spot where there is no pad, no skate, and no stick. The ball rolls in. They score.

"MY BOY. MY BOY. MY BOY."

The halftime buzzer rings. Which is good, as we could use a rest. Substitutes would be good right about now. But we have none.

But neither do they. And in the second half, Gavin shoots the ball, but no one is there to receive it. Except me.

Skates, don't fail me now. I bend my knees, pushing hard. I'm at the goalie before anyone can catch me.

He and I are almost eye-to-eye. Face-to-face

with my enemy at the moment of truth. Like Sir Chester and the Black Knight. Like Remington Reedmarsh and the Terrible Tyrant Tyler.

I pull my stick back for a hard slap shot, see my opening, and score!

"One plus one is two! One plus one is two!" Bella and Mugsy lead the cheers. I can see Dwayne doing the math on his fingers.

And two is the number of minutes we have to hold on to the lead. The clock is ticking.

"Tough D!" I yell. "Everyone back fast," I add. Meaning, we need to go help Timmy. "Don't let them score."

"What he said," comes the advice from our coach.

They take a long, hard shot at our goal. Mad Dog shoots it back. I go to get it. Gavin beats me to it. He passes it, and a teammate picks it up.

He takes a hard slap shot.

"Timmy! Incoming!" I yell louder than I did before.

"Whoooooa!" he screams as the ball flies toward him. He dives forward, his goalie glove outstretched.

And catches it!

Our coach hoots like an owl. Our fans hop around like frogs.

Timmy lies unmoving as the buzzer ends the game.

Yes!

We win!

Great!

But now what do I do?

Chapter Eight

Yeah, What She Said

"Line up. Line up," Big Buster calls both teams onto the floor. We skate past each other.

"Good game."

"Good game."

"Good game."

We mutter the words, slapping palms. The Bullfrogs mean it; the London guys don't. As Master Li says, always salute your enemy in defeat. He didn't mention anything about spitting on your palm before you slap his hand. I wipe my hand on my bullfrog's face.

Our fans rush the floor. All four of them.

"End zone dance!" Timmy cries. Freed from his goalie pads, he shows Mad Dog, Mikey, and Dwayne his standard moves.

"Hockey jersey hula!" Jack declares.

Bella and Mugsy sway to the music of "Go Bullfrogs! Go Bullfrogs!"

"Great job, Coach," my coach tells me.

"Thanks, Coach. I'm just going to put Timmy's pads away. We need all our equipment for the next game." I approach the black bag of death.

My mom moves across the floor in a most peculiar pattern. What's that? She is not dancing in front of everyone?

Before I push the pads in, I take the other things out. What to do? What to do?

Freaky Joe Rule Number Fourteen: When You Don't Know What to Do, Don't Do It.

I put them in my hockey bag.

And hula for a while. I mean, why not?

Gathering up the team and support squad takes a while.

"I am going to say this one last time," Coach Mom declares. "No one, big or small, related to me or not, will show how happy they are about this glorious victory by hitting someone else with a stick. Or a helmet. Or a glove. Or a jersey." She gives everyone a beady eye.

"If we successfully reach the car, and I do mean *if*, with no further damage to anyone's body, or to me, or my car, we will celebrate. With ice cream."

This gets us almost to the front door.

Which is blocked by the Howler, Buster, and Jamie Bowie Boudreaux; the Howler is talking, the others listening. Gavin sits nearby shredding the papers off straws.

"Would you mind making room for this parade?" my mom asks.

"It was a good game, Gavin," I tell him. He doesn't look like he's having much fun.

"It was not a good game," the Howler corrects me. "A good game is when you *win*. And I still want to know who took Gavin's gloves. Gloves don't just disappear."

She has a point there.

"I'm sure they are going to turn up. Everything will work out in the end. It always does," Miz Boudreaux tells her. "Remember, even in those dark days after the Alamo, when all looked lost . . ."

"Jamie, I love that history, but I have to get these little ones home." My mom saves us from hearing about the Battle of San Jacinto. Again. I mean, she tells it well, and it's a great story the first 124 times.

"Everything works out when you *win*. That's what I teach my boy, right, Gavin?"

"How nice for you," my mom says. "Let's go, kids." Tomorrow's headline in the paper: THE CONDOR'S MOM DECIDES TO AVOID A FIGHT.

"We're leaving," the Howler says, "but I am going to say this again. There's something fishy going on here. Equipment does not just disappear." Halfway out the door, she says loudly, "What kind of name is the Bullfrogs, anyway?"

She clearly hasn't read the chapter on amphibians in *The Big Book of Undersea Life.*

"No, you can't play with the GameBox when you get home. When you lose, you do sit-ups," are her last words as the door bangs.

Silence for a moment.

I have to say it. "Mom, I think you are great even if you are blue."

"I understand," she answers.

"I don't," Jack says.

"That is not news," Timmy tells him.

"Here's a bulletin for you." Jack swings his jersey back.

"No ice cream!" Timmy yells.

"Bullfrogs, your next game is in two nights," Buster tells us.

"We'll be ready," I promise.

"I hope so," Buster says. "You guys play the Sylvan Glen Sharks."

"The Sharks?"

"The Sharks?"

"The Sharks!"

"I think that's what I said." Buster looks a bit confused.

"Don't you think you can beat them?" Miz Boudreaux asks.

"Of course they can," Coach Mom says.

We troop out.

Bella ducks her head as we pass under the dying Alamo soldier.

Jack moans, "The Sharks!" over and over.

"We need some pinecones," Mugsy says. "And a lot of glue."

Timmy feeds Mikey and Dwayne some purple stuff he pulled from his bag.

"Interesting kind of night," my mom says.

I'll say. Any night when I agree with the Howler has to be a strange night.

But I do.

There is something fishy going on around here.

Chapter Nine

Dance the Cootie Dance

I close the book. The book. The actual Secret Files of the Freaky Joe Club.

I looked through it without finding the answer I need. I thought I might find some help here. Although it's hard to find the answer when I'm still not exactly sure of the question.

"Riley girl, this may be our most difficult case. As The Beast, you should be ready."

Riley rolls on her back and sticks all four legs up in the air. I'm hoping this is Beast talk for "You can count on me."

The door flies open with a clang. A clang because it hits the metal pie plate directly over the three-times-repaired hole in the wall. A hole that was made by banging the door straight into the wall.

"What's wrong with Riley? Is she dying? Is she only sick? Did she eat some of Timmy's food? Who's going to be the one to tell Bubba that Riley is sick? What's going on? How come we need to meet today before practice? Isn't it cool that we won last night?"

"Jack, I think you have set a new land-speed record. Eight questions and you haven't even actually come in the room."

"I'm in the room!" Timmy barrels past Jack, rolls a somersault, and leaps to his feet. "Which I think actually makes me the first one here. Oh yeah, oh yeah!"

He does a dance, which seems to be a combination of the jersey hula and the end zone dance. It's a little hard to tell since it lasts such a very short time.

"Oh yeah, well, I'm the first one to tackle someone today!" Jack leaps on Timmy. Who manages to stay on his feet.

"Oh yeah, well, I'm doing that new dance. A Jack on the back!" This dance appears to involve stumbling around while being hit on the head.

Riley thinks it's wonderful.

"No. Riley. Don't!" Jack cries. But it's too late.

Jack fell down and broke his crown, and Timmy came tumbling after.

And Riley licked them both.

"Gross! Riley, stop." Jack tries to push Riley away. She sits on his stomach. "You know, I think you can get cooties from being licked by a dog."

"Cooties aren't real," Timmy says. "Come here, Riley girl." Riley abandons Jack for Timmy. Who always has food.

"Of course cooties are real. Conor, aren't cooties real?" Jack wipes his face with his arms. "Can't we look it up in one of your books?"

Lined up on one wall of The Secret Place are the all-important books that this group of crime-solving secret agents uses in our job of being crime-solving secret agents.

"There's no time. I have an important announcement." Although I wonder if I should look under C for *cootie* or B for *bugs*.

"Look. I think my skin is dissolving where Riley licked me. Isn't that important?" Jack holds his skin one inch from his eyes.

"See any little cooties there?" Timmy asks. He and Riley are happily eating something orange.

"Why don't I stick it under your nose so you can see?" Jack looks ready to pounce.

"Secret Agents of the Freaky Joe Club!"

"Okay, okay, what announcement?" Jack asks.

"We are called to duty. We have a mystery to solve."

Jack freezes, cootied arm in midswing.

Timmy jumps up and salutes.

The Beast eats the crumbs that fall from his lap.

"This will be our third case," I remind them. "And it may be our most difficult."

"What happened? When did it happen? Why didn't you tell us last night?" Jack is in motion, fingers snapping. "I think I need a new code name for this crime."

"You don't know what the crime is," Timmy points out.

"Oh. I can feel it," Jack holds his hands out, wiggling his fingers. "It's my secret agent talent."

"Maybe it's just your fingers dissolving from cooties," Timmy suggests.

I go to my hockey bag, unzip it, and remove them.

"Gloves," Jack points out.

"Uh-oh," says Timmy.

"Gloves are uh-oh?" Jack asks.

I turn them around so they can read the word written on both gloves. *Gavin.*

"Uh-oh," Jack echoes.

"This is bad," Timmy says.

"This is a mystery," I point out.

"I have only one question," Jack declares.

Jack with only one question?

"Conor," he asks, "why did you do it?"

Chapter Ten

Meet the Evil Copycat Boy

"Jack, I didn't take Gavin's gloves." Well, not technically.

"Where did you just get them from?" Jack asks.

"From my hockey bag." I'm pointing out the obvious.

"Aha!" Jack replies. "You took *Gavin's* gloves out of *your* hockey bag."

"I think I just said that."

"Why did you put them in your hockey bag?" Jack wants to know.

"I thought I should take them out of Timmy's bag," I explain.

"Oh ho!" Jack turns on his heel, and aims a finger at Timmy. "I have just one question. Timmy, why did you do it?"

"Four," Timmy answers.

"Because he wanted four gloves, Timmy took Gavin's gloves." Jack nods his head and shakes his shoulders. "I think we can say I solved this case."

"Four questions, Jack," Timmy explains. "You said, 'I have just one question,' and you have just asked four questions."

Jack doesn't hear that answer. He's snapping his fingers, shaking his shoulders, and rapping, "Jack solved the case. Jack solved the case. Bring on the red book 'cause Jack solved the case."

"You found them in my bag? When?" Timmy asks.

"When I went to get your gloves for Gavin."

"Why didn't you give Gavin his gloves then?" Good question. It even gets Jack's attention.

"Because then everyone would have thought that you took the gloves. And the Howler would have really let loose. And we might have had to forfeit the game for cheating. And my mom might have put the Howler in a headlock. And there would have been so much noise and yelling and confusion that I might not have been able to prove right away that you didn't do it. And he had gloves, so he got to play." I think that covers it.

"Timmy didn't do it?" Jack seems so disappointed.

"Nope."

"Can you be sure?" Jack stretches out the *sure* in the most annoying way.

"Gavin waved his gloves at you and me, remember? When we were pulling Timmy up. Then I went to borrow Timmy's gloves for Gavin. Inside the bag, I saw two pairs. One of them had *Gavin* written on it."

"So?" Jack still isn't convinced.

"So, Timmy had his goalie pads on the whole time."

"Oh." Jack sees the light.

"So he couldn't move, never mind steal gloves when no one was looking."

"Sorry to disappoint you, Jack," Timmy tells him.

"It's okay," Jack answers him.

"But you did set a new land-speed record," I tell him.

"I did?"

"This is the shortest time it has ever taken you to accuse me of the crime," I point out.

"I like to try harder," Jack says.

"Here's the part I don't get," Timmy says. "How did anybody steal the gloves without someone seeing?"

"Yeah, that's exactly what I wonder too," Jack says.

"And why my bag?"

"That's the question I wanted to ask," Jack

insists, pacing and snapping his fingers.

"Oh, Copycat Boy, why don't you take a seat?" Timmy says.

"Oh, Candy Boy, how about here, on your head?" Jack suggests.

How did the gloves get in Timmy's bag? I know this is the big question. I think on it while I wait for Timmy to throw Jack off his head.

He does. Jack flies backward into me, almost knocking me down.

"That's it!" I shout.

"What's it?" asks the deadly duo.

"I know when the gloves were grabbed." Now I pace, snapping my fingers. "That should help us know who did it."

"Who's a Copycat Boy now?" Jack asks, pointing at me. Snapping his fingers.

I ignore him. I have a lot of practice at this. "We need a list." I reach for the white paper and a marker.

"Why does this always feel like homework?" Jack moans.

It takes a while (because of Jack and Riley's help) but we manage to get the paper taped to the wall. I write down my information, the important questions, and our answers.

When were the gloves put in Timmy's bag?
When the lights were out for Buster's entrance.
Who put the gloves in Timmy's bag?
Whoever skated into Conor and knocked him down. (This is why Conor found the bag half open, fallen on the floor.)
Why would someone want to take the gloves?
They wanted the London Gentlemen

to forfeit the game.

Why would they want the London Gentlemen to do that?

1) Because then the L.G. lose the game, and can't go on to the play-offs.

2) Because they don't like Gavin.

3) Because they hate listening to Gavin's mother.

4) Because they don't like the team's uniform.

"This is very good stuff," Timmy says. "Look at all these facts."

"We are sooo smart," Jack announces.

"We just need one more little piece of info," I mention.

"Which is?" Timmy asks.

"Who did it?" I answer.

"Oh, that," says Jack.

"I'm sure it was because of the Howler," Timmy insists. "Someone just snapped. His ears hurt. He couldn't take it anymore. If Gavin doesn't play, then no more yelling."

This seems like very good detective thinking to me.

"This seems like very good detective thinking to me," I tell Timmy.

"I was just going to say that," Jack tells us both.

Timmy mouths, "Copycat Boy."

"We still need to find out who," I insist. "But we have one big clue."

"We do?" Jack asks.

"We do?" Timmy echoes.

"Who's Copycat Boy now?" Jack says.

"Whoever did it was on the rink. The unknown villain skated into me and knocked me down."

"That makes it easier," Timmy says. "Because no one on their team would try and forfeit."

"But they've been listening to her at every game." Jack has a point. "Someone snapped. The brain can only take so much howling." He runs around The Secret Place, clutching his ears, moaning.

Not helpful, but well done.

He drops to the floor yelling "My ears, my ears!" The Beast tries to help him. By licking his ears.

"No, Riley!" Jack yells. "I don't want to die of cooties."

"Go get him, girl, get the evil villain Copycat Boy," Timmy urges her on.

The door clangs open. Bella comes in without knocking.

"You came in without knocking," I tell her.

"Mom says to remind you guys that practice is in one hour," Bella answers.

"Okay, okay."

"What's Jack doing?" she wants to know.

"Being a bad guy," Timmy says. "Riley is attacking him."

"I know that game," Bella says. "Mugsy plays it all the time."

"Come on, then," Timmy says. "I'm Candy Boy, who are you?"

"I like to be Brave Princess," Bella answers. Oh, there's a surprise.

"Let's do it!" Timmy and Bella pile on top of The Beast and CopyCat Boy. I realize this meeting of the Freaky Joe Club has come to an end.

I read the list over again while I wait for the others to finish. I can't help feeling that we are missing something. Could there be another reason why someone would take the gloves?

I know there is. But I don't like that answer.

Chapter Eleven

Yellow Mom Counts on One Hand

Leaving Riley behind on guard, we all leave The Secret Place. Timmy and Jack head home to get their hockey gear.

"I'll see you at the school in an hour," I say.

"We'll be there," Timmy promises, saluting as he goes. Jack is already off and running.

"Soon that school will be my school," Bella announces.

"You're right," I tell her. Bella starts kindergarten this month at the Edith R. Hammerrocker Elementary School.

Which is our school. And where the parking lot is large and smooth, perfect for running drills. And the curbs tend to keep the ball in play.

Mugsy's mom comes by to pick Bella up.

"We're going to the park," Bella tells me as she climbs in the car.

"We'll go in the trees," Mikey tells me as I click Bella's seat belt.

"And practice being gorillas at war," Dwayne adds.

"That's Mugsy's idea," Bella says as she throws me a kiss good-bye.

Mugsy just waggles her fingers at me.

Gorillas? War? In the trees?

• • • •

I head into the house to find my mom. And then it hits me, what they're talking about. My mom and I have got to talk about Mugsy.

"I am very sure that Mrs. Mara will not let the kids practice guerilla warfare at the park." My mother, who is mostly yellow today, sews something green while we talk.

"Okay, then why was Mugsy wearing a black beret?" I ask. "On a hot summer day?"

"Mugsy is a wonderfully individual child." My mother tells me something the world knows by now. "Besides, Bella can handle her."

But should my little sister have to tell her best friend that she does not want to crawl on her belly across the park to attack the swing sets? That's what I want to know.

"What are you making?" I ask.

"Oh, something for Bella. I'm just playing around. I should get back to work." She waves her hand at the painting that covers half the wall. A lot of blue, but some really good yellow.

"I need advice," I admit.

"Fire away."

"I need advice about a mystery that needs solving," I explain.

"I see. Is this official advice?" she asks. "Concerning You Know Who?"

"It is."

"Have you looked in the book?" My mom stops sewing.

"None of the cases seemed to help me," I admit.

"And does this involve gloves?"

"It does."

My mom turns off the machine. "Do we know where the gloves are?"

"In The Secret Place," I answer. "They arrived there in my hockey bag."

"Oh. Are you the one who put them in your bag?"

"I did. When I took them out of Timmy's bag," I tell her. "They went in Timmy's bag after he had his goalie pads on."

"Then Timmy couldn't have put them in the bag." She is one smart yellow mom.

"No."

"And you don't know who did?"

"No, but I know they were wearing skates."

"Well, that's one big clue," Mom realizes. She thinks quietly for a minute. "And now you're worried."

"Big worried."

"Because there is no reason one of the London Gentlemen would try and make his own team forfeit the game?"

I knew she would see the problem.

"So if it isn't someone trying to make them lose, it has to be someone trying to make us win," I say the problem out loud.

My mom holds up five fingers.

"Timmy is out. I don't believe you would do it." That's my mom.

"Big no on me," I tell her.

She folds two fingers down. "That leaves Jack, Mad Dog, and Murphy."

"But I heard Jack's voice, and Mad Dog's, away from where I was standing."

One finger left. "Do you think Murphy would do this to win?"

I have thought about this. "No, I don't."

"So, that's that," my mom says.

"But this is so frustrating. It has to be one of us," I explain. "Who else would have skated into me in the dark?"

"I believe that's what you have to discover," she points out. "Remember what's out there?"

I say the words out loud. "Freaky Joe Rule Number Eight: The Answer Is Out There Somewhere."

"Exactly." My mom stands up and brushes off

dried paint. Which still leaves her mostly blue. And yellow. "Okey dokey, I think we should return to the scene of the crime."

"Go to the rink? Why?"

"Because we don't need Gavin's gloves, do we?"

"No."

"And we don't want to call that dreadful woman and tell her we have her son's gloves, do we?"

"Solar-system-sized no."

"So we'll take the gloves and give them to Jamie Bowie Boudreaux. She can then call the Howler, who I am sure will happily cease whatever vile activity in which she is involved and come fetch the gloves. And we shall proceed on to practice."

Well, okay then.

Chapter Twelve

If You Give a Mom a Coaching Book

The Alamo is cool, dark, and almost empty. No skaters, no sticks banging on the wood floor, no howling. The sound of a machine whirring and the sight of a coonskin cap showing over the edge of side wall lead us to where Davy Crockett is cleaning the rink. Well, Jamie Bowie Boudreaux, who is today dressed in the buckskin clothes of Davy Crockett.

She sings a song loudly as she goes along. "He was born, oh yes, he was born, in the sweetest state you ever did see."

"He killed

a bar, oh yes, he was but a boy, but he killed a bar." My mother joins in loudly, raising her voice over the sound of the floor polisher. Yellow and singing. Oh boy.

"He was our own shining rocket, that daring man called Davy Crockett!" The two adults finish in unison. And they know this song how?

"How can you kill a bar?" I want to know. "Was he killed in a bar when he was but a boy? Then how did he grow up?"

"Killed him a bear," Miz Boudreaux explains. "The way Davy spoke, he would have pronounced it 'bar.'"

"How do we know what he sounded like?" I wonder. Was there a newsman reporting? *We're live here at the Alamo, and things do not look good for the defenders. I'm just going to step over and have a word with Davy Crockett.*

"We just know," she answers.

Well, okay then.

"Jamie, Conor found the missing gloves." My mother pulls them out of her backpack.

"The Howler's kid's gloves?" Miz Boudreaux looks a little confused. "How did Conor find 'em?"

"Long story. He didn't take them, he found 'em," Mom assures her.

"I know that," she tells her.

"Can you return them to that person?" my mom asks.

Miz Boudreaux sighs. "Sometimes a person has to have courage, even when it's hard. You know, it took a lot of guts for those men to stay in the Alamo." She puts her coonskin cap over her heart. "I'll call her."

"Those men would be glad to know someone remembers them so." My mother pats her on the back.

"I could talk about them all day, but now I have the floor to do. I could wait for Buster to come back and do it. But those brave men showed us we should make every day count for something. We shouldn't waste our time, or our chances. I try to do my part to help the good guys win, when I can."

"It's nice of you to feel that way. We'll see you tomorrow then. Seven-thirty?" My mom confirms the time.

"You're the second game. First the Maniac Maccabees play Joe's Kids."

"Oh, that Joe is such a nice guy," my mom says.

"Such a good kid, that Joe, a good guy," Miz Boudreaux agrees. "Of course, that's not to say you're not a good kid too," she tells me.

Well, that's a relief.

"You're just not Joe, that's all."

Well, okay then.

"I need to work. Got important things to do." The machine whirrs again. "He was born, oh yes, he was born . . . ," she sings, as loud as she can.

It's good to have this fact confirmed. Davy Crockett was born.

As we go out the front door, we bump into Buster coming in, carrying his skates. "See you tomorrow," he says. "Remember to bring your game with you. Because you will need to be ready to play some . . ."

Mom and I both rush out so we don't have to hear the rest of that.

As we arrive at the school, all the Bullfrogs are waiting.

As well as Bubba Butowski, ace security guard for Ship's Cove. The back of his security guard pickup appears to be full of dogs. Including one that looks suspiciously like The Beast.

"We're having races while we wait," Jack fills us in. "I may have broken my own land-speed record."

"But Murphy beat everybody," Timmy tells us.

"Big sister can skate." This is just a fact I know. But how bad does Big Sister want to win?

"Hey, Riley's mom," Bubba says to my mother, "the dogs just want to watch the practice. I won't let them bother anyone."

Does no one wonder how Bubba knows this?

"That will be fine, Mr. Butowski," she tells him.

I empty my hockey bag, sending the red hockey balls, marked with a C, flying around the parking lot. I keep a large supply for our practices and game warm-ups. The Bullfrogs begin to shoot them at the cones. And at each other.

My mom blows a whistle. Now where did she get that?

"Okay team, let's set these goals up, one at each end. Red cones on the side 13.4 inches apart. Take these balls down to the end. Let's go, let's go, let's go! We have a lot of work to do." Coach Mom barks the orders.

"Thirteen-point-four inches? Exactly?" I ask her. "What is up with that?"

"Master Grady Li feels that skating drills around cones that are exactly 13.4 inches apart will bring a skater greater harmony and balance. It says so on page forty-three." My mom pulls out my copy of *The Chinese Martial Arts Guide to Roller Hockey.*

"I know this stuff," I claim. I may have missed a few of the finer points.

"I sat up all last night reading this. And look at these books." Mom pulls out two more books. "*Shaka!: A Zulu Warrior Plays Roller Hockey* and *Coaching Boys: How to Make Them Play Hockey As Well As Girls.* I read them too."

I look at the books pushed under my nose.

"I'm telling you, Conor, I had no idea there was this much to coaching. I'm fascinated by the art of it. And I am ready to lead you guys to victory! To glory!"

"This is just the championships of the Siege of the Alamo Summer Hockey League," I remind her.

"Yes, but a thing worth doing is worth doing well," she answers.

"Who said that, Master Li?" I ask.

"Great-grandmother Bridget," she answers. "And we know how smart she was. Besides, the trophy's not bad either." She holds her hand off the ground to show how big it is.

"Trophy size!" Jack yells over. He is lying on the ground. Murphy measures the distance from his elbow to his armpit. Timmy and Mad Dog pick him up, lay him down, and they measure again.

Oh, good. Math and Hockey practice.

• • • •

We try all my mother's drills. They are mostly odd.

"I thought you were our coach, Conor," Jack says. "And your mom just helped."

"That was the plan. I'm not sure when it changed," I confess.

"I think she has interesting ideas." Murphy takes the coach's side.

"I don't know," Timmy says. "I'm not sure how doing the Zulu spear dance on skates helps us."

"I'm not sure either, but the dogs seemed to like that one best," I admit.

"Riley girl is such a good girl staying in the truck," Timmy says.

"That's just because she can't eat my flesh with all this padding on," Jack insists.

"I liked that one she called Chasing the Hun from the Great Wall of China," Mad Dog adds.

"Well, that's because it had a lot of growling," Murphy says.

"All righty, team, this is the last drill," Coach Mom yells. "One at a time, I want you to skate as hard as you can down the parking lot, and when you are at full speed I want you to balance on one foot, and score a goal. Find your center, be one with the ball, and you *will* score. Okay, let's roll." A whistle, again.

"I can so do this," Jack says.

He can't.

"Where's my center?" Timmy asks.

"Where you keep your candy," I tell him.

A few more tries.

"Oh, Mad Dog, that looks bad. Maybe we should mop up the blood before the next skater." Mom is a concerned coach.

It's my turn. I actually think I can

do this. Skating on one foot is my thing.

I set off. Full speed. Control the ball, keep going, now balance, I'm on one foot, I'm going to make it, I take a shot. . . .

The whistle blows loud near my ear, distracting me. But I'm still on the ball.

It was one whistle too many. The dogs decide to join the practice. Riley decides to help me.

I cannot be one with the ball when it is in Riley's mouth.

"Oh well, good try, sport," the whistle blower shouts. Sport?

"Come on, doggies, good doggies, no more playing," Bubba calls. "Who wants a treat? No one gets a treat unless they are in Uncle Bubba's truck."

And that takes care of the dog problem. I honestly didn't know toy poodles could jump that high.

"Okay team, that'll do," our strange coach

announces. "The other team, Joe's Kids, is here to use the parking lot."

It's great that Joe's Kids are in the play-offs. And a little surprising.

Joe is a high school student who always coaches a team. It's a team made up of stragglers, kids from neighborhoods that don't have their own team, or kids who are so awful they are banished from their neighborhood team. Imagine a whole team of Dwaynes. That's Joe's Kids.

And he plays every kid every game, no matter what, even though a few of his kids have trouble standing in skates. And he always manages to pull a few wins out of their helmets.

Joe's a good guy.

He shakes my mom's hand. "Good luck tomorrow. Maybe we'll meet in the finals."

"We'll see you there," Mom answers. "Okay, Bullfrogs, let's ride."

"Ride what?" Jack asks. "I've got skates on."

"Okay, kids, all at once," Joe lifts his hand like a conductor.

"GOOD LUCK TOMORROW, BULLFROGS," Joe's kids call out.

I mean, nice kids. Several of them even manage to remain upright.

Oh, boy. Tomorrow they have to play the Maniac Maccabees from the Jewish community center.

Not looking good for Joe's Kids.

Chapter Thirteen

Take a Ride in the Swamp Mobile

"I love this car so much," Jack tells my mom again.

"Everyone wishes they were in our car," Bella says.

Not everyone. Some of us *in* the car wish we were not.

"How did you make the bullfrog?" Timmy asks. That would be the very large bullfrog sitting on the roof of our big green sorta car, sorta truck. It's sitting on vines that run down the sides, stopping above the words SWAMP MOBILE and GO BULLFROGS.

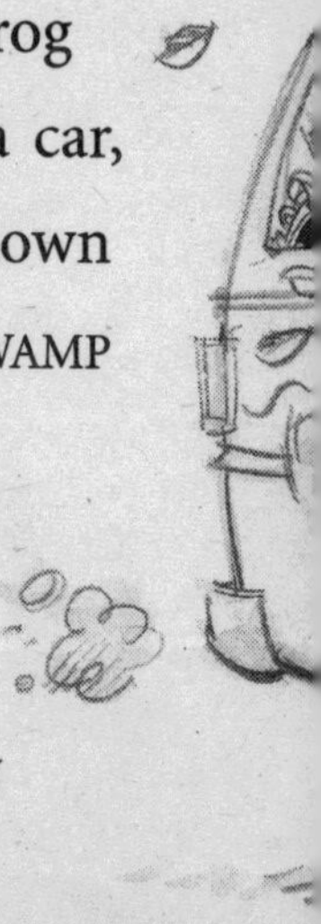

"Newspaper, plaster of Paris, a little of this and that," my mom answers.

"We helped," the four fans, who are now

clearly going to every game, answer. No one would have guessed that. I mean, aren't small children mostly green? And wearing frog heads made from green material? *What are you sewing, Mom? Oh nothing. Just frog heads for your next game.*

"Does everyone know that bullfrogs are cannibals who will sometimes eat their own family?" Mugsy asks. She gives her brother a big smile and a big chomp of the teeth.

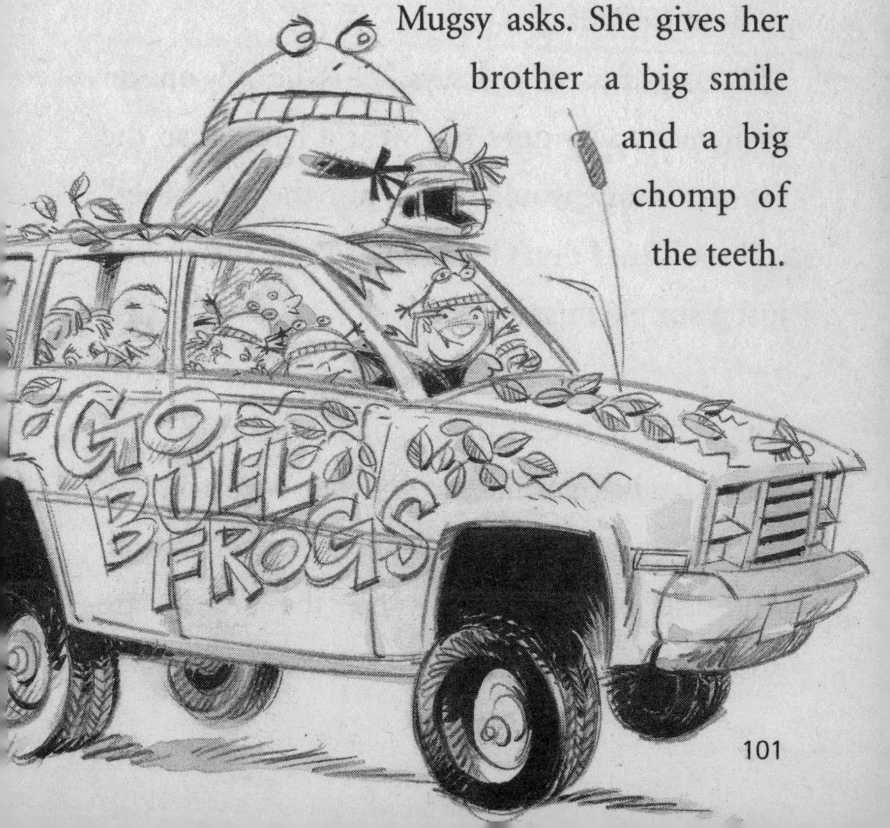

"Noooo!" Mikey cries.

Dwayne rolls up in a ball.

"Then maybe your mom will eat you," Bella tells Mugsy.

"You know, we never finished talking about Gavin's gloves," Timmy reminds me. "We still don't know who took them."

"I say it was Tony, their coach," Jack declares.

"Because?" I ask.

"Beeccaauussee," Jack says, "he is the only one on their team who does not wear a helmet, so the Howler's noise would bother him the most. See?"

"I see." But I don't believe it. Maybe this was all just a simple mistake?

The game between the Maniac Maccabees and Joe's Kids has a minute to go when we arrive. We throw our gear down in a pile by the back wall. And the other pile tells me the Sharks are already here.

Timmy reads the scoreboard aloud. "Joe's Kids three, Maccabees two."

"Way to go, Kids!" That Joe can coach.

"Still anyone's game," Mad Dog says as he finds us in the crowd of cheering fans and teams waiting to play. Jeremiah of the Sharks points at me and draws his hand across his throat. Oh, nice.

"Joe's Kids can hold on," I say. I hope.

"But the Maccabees have Benny the Bomber," Mad Dog points out.

"Oh, man, he can shoot," Timmy says.

"Not to mention Ruby. Little sister can skate," I remind them.

Benny the Bomber steals the ball and slaps it hard, a good pass to his little sister. Ruby skates fast toward the other goal.

It's Ruby vs. Jeffy, Joe's goalie.

"Come out," Joe yells. "Cut the corners, cut the angle."

Jeffy gets brave, moves out from the goal. Ruby shoots.

Jeffy drops. And blocks.

The clock stops. The Maccabees call a time out.

"What would Shaka Zulu do now?" my mom asks.

Big Buster skates off to confer with Miz Boudreaux in the announcer's booth.

And then a face-off again. Ruby takes this one. She passes to Benny. He makes a run toward the goal, skating his way through the defenders.

Every single eye is on the skater. Maccabees supporters are going nuts. Joe's Kids fans are going nuts.

Benny brings his stick back. Oh man, he is going to score. He shoots hard. Then the ball rolls sideways, in a kind of loopy loop. And completely misses the goal.

The buzzer sounds. Game over.

Benny the Bomber can't believe it. He throws his stick on the ground in the time-honored tradition of frustrated hockey players. Ruby stamps her feet. Well, her skates.

But Joe's Kids win.

We wait on the floor while the teams slap hands and gather their gear. The Sharks do too.

"Hey, Bullfrogs, ready to be eaten by a Shark?" our old friend Jeremiah yells over at us.

"Yeah! Eaten," says Jake. He still has a way with words.

"Can you believe Benny missed that shot?"

Mick the Shark asks. "I mean that kid has one mean slap shot."

"Who cares?" Jeremiah says. "Let's go wipe the floor with these guys."

"Master Li would not approve of such talk," my mother tells him. Oh, boy. "He would say you are ruining the harmony of this game."

"Huh?" Jake asks.

"Watch what you say," my mom explains. "I can have you removed from the game for bad sportsmanship. So wipe the floor with that."

"Wow! Who's that?" Murphy interrupts.

"What's that?" would be a better question. A large, square, boylike shape moves slowly across the rink.

"Our goalie," Jeremiah says happily. "You haven't met Ludivico; he's not on the swim team."

That would be because there would be no

water left after he dived in. He's one big kid.

"Holy Moly," Mad Dog says.

"Yeah, whatever that means," Jack says.

"We're goners," Timmy says.

Chapter Fourteen

How's That Song Go?

I've had enough. "We are not goners. We are Bullfrogs, the largest frog found in North America. We are fast, we are mean, we are cannibals who eat anyone who gets in our way. Our cry can be heard at night across the swamps and bayous. A unique cry, telling those we prey on to be afraid, very afraid. Bullfrogs are out tonight!"

"Yeah!"

"Bullfrogs."

"We're bad, we're mean."

"And we don't say 'ribbit,'" I add. "No silly little frog noise. Scientists have studied our call. They have recorded it. Any herpetologist can tell you that we say 'jug-o-rum, jug-o-rum.' And that cry causes fear. Say it loud and say it proud, Bullfrogs!"

"Bullfrogs!"

"Jug-o-rum!"

"Bullfrogs!"

"Jug-o-rum!"

"Now let's get our gear on and win this hockey game," I tell them.

"Yeah!"

I don't tell them I have no idea how we are going to score goals when it appears that Ludivico covers every inch of space in front of the net. Impressive.

Big Buster's voice comes over the loudspeaker. "It's almost time for some hoooccckkkeeey!"

I take the practice balls from the bag. We skate, shoot. Mom wheels Timmy into place. We try to score on him. He tries to stop us. At the other end, Ludivico guards the

goal. Who can get past that monster?

A Bullfrog can, I remind myself.

Big Buster skates around. "Ready for inspection?"

I collect our practice gear, scooping up the balls with the big C on them. One of them lies over in the corner of the rink. Practicing a side stop, I pick it up. I don't see the C, but mine are the only ones out here. I've picked up a few strays along the way, and I'm pretty sure there are some of mine rolling around in other players' bags. This one can join our team for now.

Skating to the bench, I almost run into Buster. Buster? He was on the rink in the dark. He could have taken the gloves. Why would Buster care who wins? Could Buster have been trying to help us out?

The lights begin to dim. Great. Now I have to find my gear in the dark.

The disco light comes on.

Buster comes out. Asks his question again. And again. And again.

The Sharks skate out when he calls their name. Ludivico carries their coach on one shoulder.

"Jug-o-rum! Jug-o-rum!" our green frog fans call when we are introduced.

"Inspection," Buster announces.

"Huddle," calls Mom, who missed the parts of the books that explain the difference between this sport and football.

"They are big boys," she points out. "A little bit scary."

Not helping, Mom.

"But we are trained, we are focused, we are centered, we are ready."

Okay, that's better.

"Timmy, look at that big guy," I say, pointing at the goalie. "He's huge. And he loves candy. He can't get enough for himself. Oh no, he needs other people's candy. He needs yours," I say. "And if he wins, he's coming to get it."

"Then they can't win, can they?" Timmy's eyes get that nice red glow I was hoping for.

"Jack, the Sharks think you're strange, you know that. Show them you are strange *and* fast. Mad Dog, please act like one. We all know you can. Murphy, I have only one favor to ask."

"You got it," she says.

"Make them wish they had a girl on their team."

The Sharks begin to line up.

"Where's my stick?" Jeremiah yells.

Not again.

They would have a problem if Jeremiah can't play. He's their best player, far and away. "Who took my stick?" he yells louder.

"Hold your horses, kid." Jamie Bowie Boudreaux comes out, carrying a stick. "I found this up against the wall. Your name Jeremiah?"

She carries it across to the Sharks.

Okay, so we don't have a stolen stick situation. What we have is a hockey game to win.

To me, a good hockey game is like that thing, the pendulum, hanging on the bottom of a big clock. It swings back and forth, back and forth. Our side of the rink, then theirs. We have the ball, they do.

Someone scores! Oh no. Okay, let's do it some more.

Unless one team rolls all over the other, and the ball stays at one end.

This is not that kind of game.

Back and forth, back and forth it goes.

Except no one scores.

We cannot seem to find even a sliver of space around Ludivico to get our ball in the net.

We try. It always seems to hit that silver shark jersey, or the silver shark pants with the blood

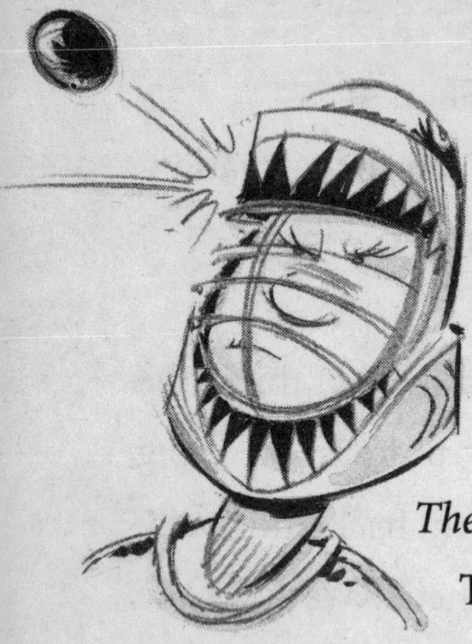

dripping down the leg. Once it bounced off his helmet. That would be the helmet painted on top to look like the inside of a shark's mouth. I need to check in *The Big Book of Undersea Life.* They can't possibly have that many teeth.

The Sharks try too. But our goalie is on fire.

"Get your own candy," he screams anytime anyone comes near the goal. Between Timmy and Mad Dog, who appears to be foaming at the mouth, the Sharks come up empty.

It does not help them that Jeremiah appears to be having the worst game of his life.

I can hear their coach discussing this with him at halftime. Actually, the lemurs on Henderson Island could hear him.

"WHAT IS YOUR PROBLEM, KID? YOU

HAVEN'T CONNECTED WITH THE BALL ALL NIGHT. DO YOU NOT KNOW THIS IS A BIG GAME? HAVE YOU FORGOTTEN HOW TO PLAY HOCKEY?"

We have got to introduce this guy to the Howler.

"I don't know what's up. I'll rip them apart in the second half." Jeremiah is not a happy guy.

"Yeah. Rip apart," Jake says.

But he doesn't. He tries; they all do, but they can't get past the deadly duo of Candy Boy and Mad Dog.

We try, but we can't get past the snarling, drooling, Monster Boy Ludivico.

And then there are only two minutes left.

Mad Dog shoots the ball back down the rink. I take it. Look around. Heads up is the way to play hockey.

Murphy bangs her stick on the floor. She's ahead of Jake. I pass. She gets it. Skates fast. Jake sprints. She's faster. Gets to the goal all alone.

To face the giant Ludivico. "What you gonna do, Girlie?" He laughs in her face.

Skate right is what she is going to do. He turns. She turns back again, like lightning. He can't. What she is going to do is cross the net in front of him. And skate right up to the goal. And find the tiny sliver of space between his left skate and the post. And lift the ball in!

"What Girlie is going to do is score on you!"

The team goes wild. The frogs go crazy. They jump higher than a frog has ever jumped before.

But the game is not over. Another face-off. Mick wins it, and shoots the ball down to Jeremiah. He races to the goal, teaching Mad Dog a lesson about dribbling as he passes him by.

It's Jeremiah vs. Timmy.

"Timmy, come out," I scream. "Cut his angle."

Timmy actually moves on his own. Faces Jeremiah. And begins to lift his legs up and down. Stomps his feet up and down.

What is he doing?

"Shaka!" he cries.

Jeremiah takes a slap shot. Timmy goes down.

And Jeremiah misses. The ball just rolls over the top of his stick. Amazing that he would miss. But it was a good thing, as Timmy has fallen over doing his Zulu spear dance.

The buzzer sounds. The Bullfrogs win!

Jeremiah yells. It's not a nice word. He throws his stick down and skates off.

"Jug-o-rum! Jug-o-rum!" The Bullfrogs race across the rink shouting and throw themselves on top of Timmy. The frog fans join in.

The Sharks stand frozen.

"What?" Jake asks, his mouth hanging open.

"We lost," Mick tells him.

"I don't know what that means," he says.

"You're good," I tell him. "But we're weird. Weird wins."

Happy that I have been able to help Jake learn something new, I skate to join the pileup. And to tell my mom to stop doing whatever that dance is she's doing.

I run into Jeremiah's stick and almost go flying. I decide to be a nice guy. Picking it up, I try to return it.

"Good game," I tell him.

"NOT A GOOD GAME," he screams into my face. I think Master Li might say this is not the proper spirit in which to accept defeat.

"Your stick." I try to hand it to him.

"I don't ever want to see that stick again!" He turns his back.

Well, okay then.

I try to give Jeremiah's stick to Miz Boudreaux, but she doesn't want it either. So I take it along

when we load up into the car. No reason to throw away a perfectly good stick. At the least, we can use it to decorate the walls of The Secret Place. Hang it up next to the ripped SQUISH THE FISH poster.

"All right, Bullfrogs!" Coach Mom cries. "On to ice cream! And tomorrow night the Championship!"

There's only one problem with that, I realize.

To win, we have to beat Joe's Kids.

And who wants to do that?

Well, the Sharks would.

And the Maniac Maccabees.

And the London Gentlemen.

Okay, who in this car would want to beat Joe's Kids?

I hope the answer to that is no one.

And that it has nothing to do with Gavin's gloves.

Chapter Fifteen

The Last Battle at the Alamo

"But Lady Beatrice the Beautiful could never have poisoned the king," Sir Chester is telling his squire, Chuck. "Such a winsome maiden would ne'er do such a vile deed."

"Sir Chester, Sir Chester." Chuck shaketh his head. "You do need to see the clues here laid out before ye."

"Conor, oh Conor," a voice calleth to me. "What are you waiting for?"

Bella sticks her face right in mine, over the top of the book.

"Mom is ready to go. She's in the Swamp Mobile."

Holy Moly. I came out to put on my skates and

picked up the third Sir Chester book for one minute. A while ago.

"Bella, carry my skates. I'll put them on at the rink." I grab my gear, mark my place in the book, pull my bag on my shoulder, and race to the car. Everyone's here. Some of us are green. Including my mother, but I don't have time to think about that. We are off to the game that really is a Big Game.

In the car Bella, Mugsy, and Jack see if they can turn greener by holding their breath. Timmy and Mikey eat sorta green jellybeans. Murphy thumb wrestles with Dwayne, letting him win.

"Be one with the game, be one with the game," my mom chants.

I just know no one in the Swamp Mobile took Gavin's gloves. There probably is no mystery here, I realize. Just some guy on Gavin's team playing a goofy trick, and then not wanting to get caught. I mean, nothing else has happened. Right?

• • • •

"Conor, can you get Timmy ready and then put your skates on? I'll just settle the little frogs in one place."

"Got it. Hey, Miz Boudreaux," I call as I cross the rink. "You really look like Jim Bowie." Can't hurt to be nice. "I'll be back for my skates in a minute."

"Don't worry," she tells me.

With his pads on, I push Timmy into place.

"These guys are good guys. They have their own candy," I assure him.

"Roger."

I throw the practice balls out of my bag for the team. They shoot, Timmy blocks. Now, where did I leave my skates? Great, they're not on the bench where I left them.

Mugsy is where? I see her with my mom. And then I spy my skates behind one of the benches. Someone must have knocked them over. I break the land-speed record for lacing.

Grabbing my stick, I head to take some shots on Timmy. The stick feels all wrong. Oh great, I grabbed Jeremiah's. Good thing The Condor always comes prepared. I always take extra sticks to a game.

"Incoming," Jack yells. He aims a slap shot at me.

"Got it!" I shoot the ball back. Except I don't. The ball jumps right over the stick.

"Try again," Murphy yells. She sends one my way. I hit it back. Except I don't. I miss it.

"Better calm down before the game," Mom calls. She puts her arms out to the side. "Say it with me! Ommm. Ommm."

I don't think so. But what's up with me? I swipe at a ball near the bench. And miss.

It must be an unlucky stick.

This does not make sense. Bella would say it was under a spell from an evil queen. Mugsy would say it was a plot. Mugsy would probably be responsible for the plot.

A plot? Remember Freaky Joe Rule Number Twenty-Four: If It Doesn't Make Sense, It Doesn't. Okay, what's wrong with this stick?

I hold two sticks, mine and his, side by side. Jeremiah's is taller, but that's 'cause he is. Your hockey stick has to fit you. I turn them upside down. And say "Aha!"

Rough edges. All along the bottom of Jeremiah's. Where it has been recently cut. Making a thinner blade. Making it easier for a ball to jump over when someone swings the stick. Which makes it harder to score.

Who is trying to make sure the Bullfrogs win?

Who doesn't think we can win on our own?

I pull the words up in my memory. "If you can?" and "Think you can?"

Buster doesn't think we can win. Buster is trying to help us win. But why?

I don't care why. We don't need his help. We can win all on our own. But can we? We beat the London guys fair and square. But could we beat the Sharks if Jeremiah was scoring?

"The game will start in two minutes," Buster announces.

"Deep in the Heart of Texas" starts playing over the PA.

I have to fix this. I cross the floor, skipping around a ball Jack sends loopy loop across the floor.

"Buster, can I say something?"

He turns from fiddling with the PA system. "Go ahead."

"The Bullfrogs can win tonight," I say. "We don't need help to win. We didn't need help any other night to win. I hope no one tries to help us tonight."

Buster looks at me like I have two heads and both are up my armpits. "Well, I hope so! Are you saying someone is cheating? Because anyone who cheats in a hockey game is a no-good, low-down, yellow-bellied, lily-livered coward who does not deserve to play this game." Buster stands over me and leans down. "Is there something you're trying to tell me?"

"Nope. I just wanted to tell you we are ready to play some hockey."

"That's the spirit! I'm just getting ready to start the disco ball."

Miz Boudreaux skates over. "Everything okay?" she asks.

"No worries," I tell her. Maybe I have no worries.

But I have big confusion. Unless he's the best actor in the world, I was wrong about Buster. Okay, then maybe I'm wrong about the gloves, and the stick. Maybe I'm not the secret agent I think I am. Maybe Freaky Joe would not be happy that I am the one who has the book. Maybe I should . . .

"Duck, Conor," Murphy calls. Practicing lifting the ball, she has lifted a little too high. I skirt round Mad Dog's shot and avoid another loopy loop by Jack. He's off his game. And that's not good.

"Jack," my mom calls, "ommm. Ommm."

I should redo my laces. I must not have tied them tight enough when I rushed. My skates feel funny. But there's no time left.

No one is missing gloves, sticks, helmets, anything. So we start. It's a pendulum game back and forth, the way I like it.

But at the half, they are ahead by one.

"What could I do?" Timmy asks. "Did you see that cute little kid? He fell down in front of me. So I helped him up. And he shot around me."

"Don't worry, lots of time to win, lots of time," my mom says.

But the clock is running down. We have to make something happen. I should tighten my laces; I feel wobbly. *Never mind,* I tell myself. *Focus on the game.*

Jack gets the ball. I hope this one doesn't go loopy. Go loopy??? Like Benny's! Oh man, Conor! It's not just the Bullfrogs. Someone is trying to make sure Joe's Kids win too. But that doesn't make sense. Why help two teams?

Mad Dog blocks a ball in front of the goal, then shoots it down to the other end.

I skate for it, trying hard to figure this out. Someone wanted Joe's Kids to play the Bullfrogs in the championship? That's the only way this makes sense. But why? I mean, we're both good teams. Well, we're both okay teams. But we're both good guys.

That's it!

Okay, if that's the deal, then we'll have no more trouble. Anyone can win tonight.

"I got it!" Jack gets to the ball first. He passes it to Murphy.

"Murphy." I bang my stick. She sends it my way. I get it. And a clear path to the goal. One of Joe's Kids is right behind me. I pick up speed. I'm on a breakaway. One-on-one, me against the goalie. I am going to score.

Whoa, what's up! I am going to fall! The goal is in front of me but one of my wheels is flying behind me.

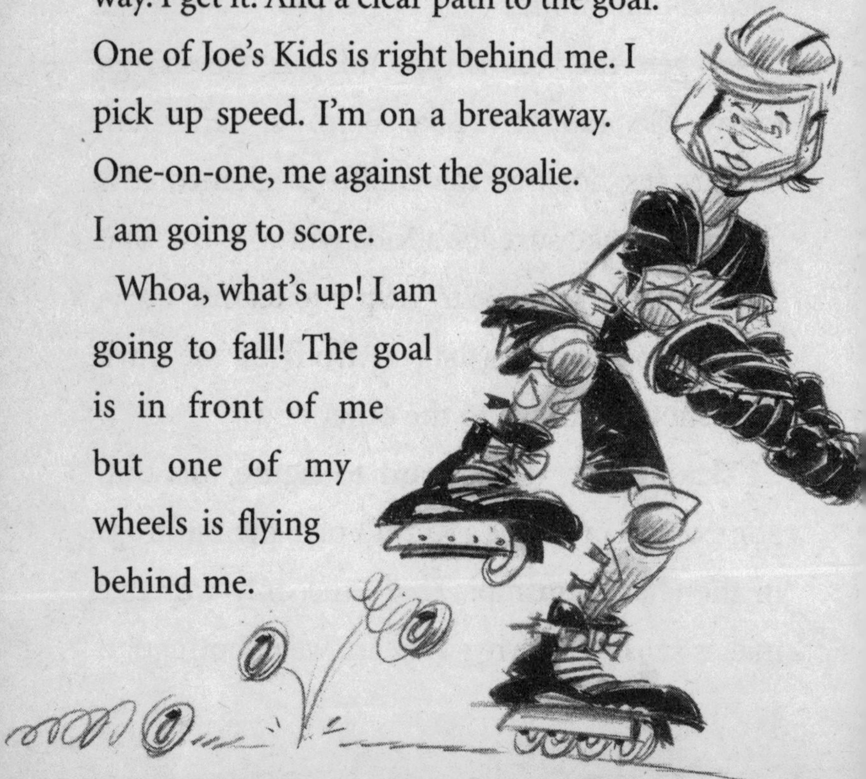

"Incoming!" Mugsy yells.

I have only three wheels on one skate.

"Time out!" my mother cries. Other voices yell, cry, I don't know what.

Another wheel flies away.

I don't fall. I'm still going forward. And I still have the ball.

I can do this. I balance on one foot as a third wheel falls off. Glide forward to a new one-legged skate-speed record. I shoot. And put it in the net.

"Goal!" someone yells.

I keep going, bounce off the goal post, then plow into the nearest wall. *Bang!*

At the same time the buzzer goes off. Game over!

Joe yells, "Hooray! A tie!"

I feel pain in more than one place.

"Conor, say something!" My mother looks worried.

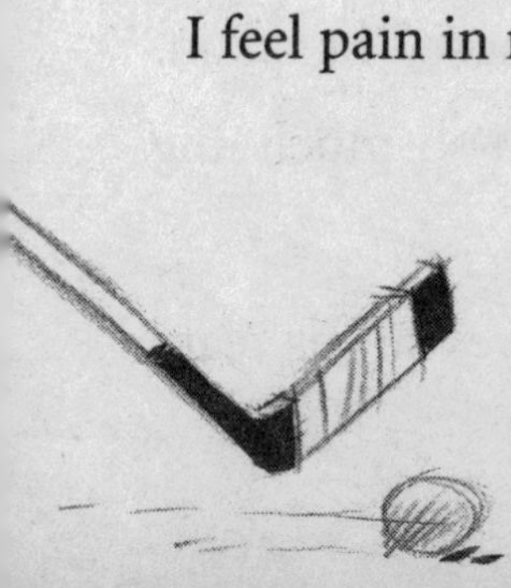

She leans over me, surrounded by Bullfrogs and little frogs.

"Jug-o-rum?"

"Are you okay, can you get up?"

"If Murphy and Mad Dog get off my legs."

"He's okay?" Joe asks in a worried voice. He's a nice guy.

"That was simply amazing, kid," Buster tells me. "That's one of the greatest moments in the history of roller hockey. But here's a little safety tip: Always remember to check your wheels before a game."

"I always remember to check my wheels before a game," I say.

"Then how did they fly off, Hockey Boy?" Jack asks.

"'Cause someone made them loose," I explain.

"Then that someone is in oh-so-much big trouble." My mom means it.

"And someone hid Gavin's gloves so his team

would have to forfeit. And someone cut Jeremiah's stick, making it too thin, so when he took a shot, the ball would bounce right over the top."

"Now there's a good idea," Timmy says. "Not that I would try it."

"I would," Mugsy says.

"That's not all. I think if you look in my bag, there is at least one practice ball without a C. I'll bet we find it's been cut somehow so it's uneven. Which makes it roll funny. Makes it go loopy loop."

"So the Jack man was not at fault today. I knew I was too good to hit like that." Jack pats himself on the back.

"Why would someone do that?" my mom and Timmy ask at the same time.

"To make sure the Bullfrogs would play Joe's Kids in the final," I explain. I'm so sure I'm right.

"Why would someone do that?" Buster asked.

"No offense, but you guys are not the toughest players in the league. I mean, you're great kids and all . . ."

"Yup," I say, "we're good guys."

"Good guys? Good guys!" I can see my mom get it.

"I try to do my part to help the good guys win," I say.

Yes, we've heard those words before.

"Well, what is so wrong with that?" Miz Boudreaux asks. "That just one time, the championship should go to the sweetest coach with the nicest kids in the league?"

"Oh, I could come up with a long list of what is wrong with that." My mom is rolling up her sleeves.

I stop her. "As someone once said, it is a bad idea to do a bad thing for a good reason."

"Did You Know Who say that?" Timmy asks.

"I don't think so," my mom says. "Did You Know Who say that?" she asks me.

"I thought you were You Know Who," Timmy says.

"Who knows who?" Jack asks.

"I'm confused," Buster says.

"Join the club," Jack says. "Only not our club."

"I'm not You Know Who," my mom tells Timmy. "But I'm honored you would think so."

"Actually, forget that," Jack tells Buster. "We have no club. Right, everyone? No club. No You Know Who."

"Well, if you are not You Know Who, how do you know about You Know What?" Timmy is now Question Boy.

"Is You Know Who, You Know Who?" Jack asks.

Stop the madness is what I think.

"Jug-o-rum! Jug-o-rum!" is what our fans yell as they run around the rink riding hockey sticks as horses.

"I don't know about who knows what," Buster says. "But what I do want to know is, are you ready to play some hockey? We've got to break this tie! And we've got some trophies waiting to be held overhead while you skate a victory lap!"

"Not right now, Buster," my mom says. "I think we have all had enough hockey for one night."

"Enough hockey? Enough hockey?" Clearly this is an idea that has never occurred to Buster.

"I want to go lie down," Miz Boudreaux announces. "You know, Jim Bowie was fighting from his bed when the Alamo fell."

"I think that's a good idea," Mom says. "I think you definitely have had too much hockey."

"I have another good idea," Joe says. "Listen. . . ."

• • • •

And that is almost the very end of this Freaky Joe Club's third case. At Joe's suggestion, the championship was replayed in the parking lot of the Edith R. Hammerrocker Elementary School. From the beginning.

The Bullfrogs played the London Gentlemen. And the Howler howled. And Gavin had his gloves. And we still won.

The Maniac Maccabees played with Ruby but no Benny, who had already gone to Hebrew camp. Joe's Kids won.

"But you'll never know if you could beat them if Benny was playing," Jack worried.

"Don't care," Joe answered. "This is fun for now."

Jeremiah didn't show when we played the Sharks. He says he is never playing again. Not my problem. But this was my game. Big brother can skate. We won.

In the finals, the Bullfrogs played Joe's Kids. And big sister can skate. We won.

Then we gave Joe's Kids the trophies.

The Bullfrogs decided they were too big. Really. We only had to pry one out of Jack's hands.

Miz Boudreaux sold the hockey rink to Buster. And went to work as a tour guide at the wax muse-um across from the Alamo.

But right now, you can't pry the fourth Sir Chester book out of my hands. I have a good mystery to read, and only a week before school starts.

This will be a good day.

And if you are looking for another good day, don't forget to read THE FREAKY JOE CLUB SECRET FILE #4
The Case of the Walking Computer
Coming soon to a bookstore or library near you